Mum and Dad are going to see a film. Liz comes to look after Beth and Alex. "They must go to bed at seven," says Mum.

Beth and Alex have wooden bunk
beds. Liz tucks them up.
"Read us a book!" says Alex.

Liz ends up reading six books.

"Sing us a song!" says Beth.

"Just one song," says Liz. But she ends up singing six songs.

Liz is having a cup of coffee. In comes Beth.

"My doll fell out of bed," she says. "Will you kiss her foot?"

Liz kisses the doll's foot. Then, "Back to bed," she says.

Liz has a sip of coffee. In comes Alex. He has hiccups.

Liz gives Alex a drink. Then,
"Back to bed," she says.

In comes Beth. "Alex is jumping on the bed," she says.

"Back to bed, Alex," says Liz.

Alex comes in. "Beth has got Mum's lipstick," he says.

"BACK TO BED!" Liz yells.

Mum and Dad come back.
"Was the film good?" says Liz.

"Yes," says Dad. "And were Beth and Alex good?"

"Yes!" says Liz.